leisure & culture DUNDEE

This SCRIBBLERS

book belongs to:

....

Stratford
Upon Avon Literary Festival
Salariya
Picture Book Prize

The Salariya Book Company partners with the Stratford-upon-Avon Literary Festival in an annual prize to find the next big children's author/illustrator. Since the prize began in 2017, winners have had their debut picture book published by Salariya. *Snow?* was selected from the final shortlist of titles to win the prize.

The judges:

Philip Ardagh is the award-winning author of titles including *The Grunts* and *Grubtown Tales*.

Annie Ashworth is the Director of the Stratford-Upon-Avon Literary Festival.

Rob Biddulph is the award-winning author and illustrator of titles including *Odd Dog Out* and *Sunk!*

Jane Churchill is a highly experienced children's book events programmer.

Jodie Hodges is a literary agent representing authors and illustrators of children's books.

Tamsin Rosewell is a broadcaster and bookseller at Kenilworth Books, an acclaimed independent bookshop.

David Salariya is a designer, author and the founder and Managing Director of The Salariya Book Company and its imprints Book House, Scribblers and Scribo.

About the author and illustrator: Joanne Surman has a Masters in Illustration and has worked in many spheres of the design industry including animation for computer games, children's television (BBC and Channel 4), and interactive software design for heritage sites (National Trust and museums). She is now a full-time illustrator of children's books.

For Jacob and Olivia, with all my love and gratitude for making every moment special.

Jo

This edition published in Great Britain in MMXXII
by Scribblers, an imprint of
The Salariya Book Company Ltd
25 Marlborough Place,
Brighton BN1 1UB
www.salariya.com

SALARIYA
SCRIBO BOOK HOUSE SCRIBBLERS

HB ISBN-13: 978-1-913971-10-6

1 3 5 7 9 8 6 4 2

A CIP catalogue record for this book is available from the British Library.

Printed and bound in China.

Printed on paper from sustainable sources.

Visit
www.salariya.com
for our online catalogue and
free fun stuff.

Snow?

Jo Surman

SCRIBBLERS
a SALARIYA *imprint*

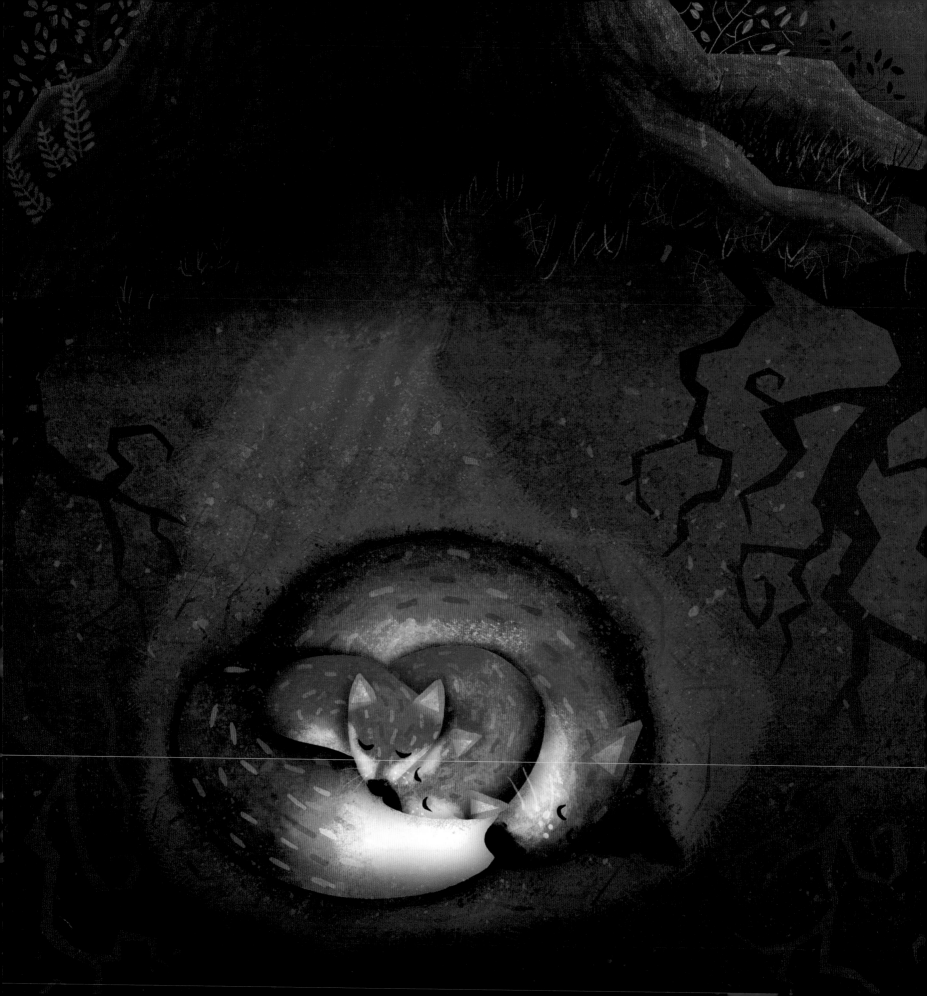

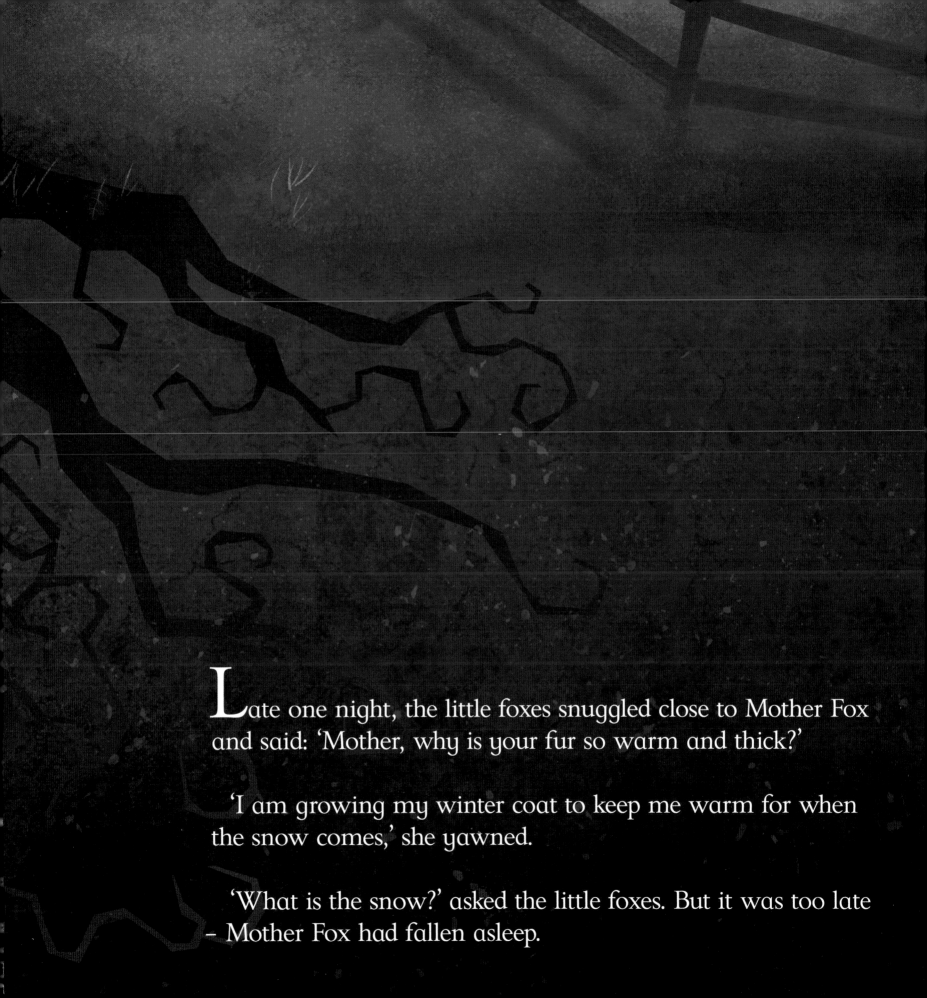

Late one night, the little foxes snuggled close to Mother Fox and said: 'Mother, why is your fur so warm and thick?'

'I am growing my winter coat to keep me warm for when the snow comes,' she yawned.

'What is the snow?' asked the little foxes. But it was too late – Mother Fox had fallen asleep.

The next morning, Mother Fox left the cubs alone in the cosy den to go searching for food, so the little foxes scampered out to find someone who could tell them what this 'snow' was.

'Squirrel, squirrel,' asked the little foxes, 'can you tell us what snow is?'

'I'm far too busy,' said the squirrel, in a hurry. 'I'm gathering nuts to store, because when the snow comes there will be no more food on the freezing ground and nothing to eat. Goodbye!'

'Oh! So snow makes food disappear!' said the little foxes.

'Little bird, little bird,' asked the little foxes,
'can you tell us what snow is?'
The little bird fluttered his wings and shivered.
'I can't stop now,' he said. 'It will be coming
soon and it will be too cold for me, so I'm flying
off to a warmer country. But I'll be back in spring.
Goodbye.' And off he flew.

Down came an owl, huffing and puffing. 'Owl, owl,' asked the little foxes, 'can you tell us what snow is?'

'Oh,' huffed the owl. 'Can't stop! I've just flown here from far away – the cold is just right for me now, but I need to find a place to nest before the snow comes.' And she swooped away.

'So snow makes food disappear and it's very cold?' said the little foxes.

'Hedgehog, hedgehog,' asked the little foxes, 'can you tell us what snow is?'

Nuzzling into his nest of leaves, the hedgehog replied, 'I'm too busy, little foxes. It's coming, and when it falls it will cover the ground, so I need to be safely tucked up so I can hibernate through till spring. Goodbye!'

And with that, he curled into a ball, shut his eyes and fell into a *deep* sleep.

'Little mice, little mice,' asked the little foxes, 'can you tell us what snow is?

'We're in a terrible hurry,' replied the dormice. 'We also hibernate, so we must gather as much grass as possible to keep us warm.'

And with that, they snuggled up close and pulled the grass around them.

'So snow makes food disappear, it's very cold, it falls from the sky and covers the ground?' said the little foxes to each other, and hurried along to find someone else to tell them more.

'Mole, mole,' asked the foxes, 'can you tell us what snow is?'

'I wish I had more time,' said mole, brushing soil from her nose. 'But it will be coming soon and I need to practise my digging skills. It makes the ground so hard and frozen, and I must dig much deeper where it's warmer whilst I wait for spring.'

And with that she was gone...

deep,

deep

underground.

'So snow makes food disappear, it's very cold,
it falls from the sky and covers the ground and
makes it hard?' Excited now, the little foxes
hurried along to find someone else who could
tell them more.

'Bumblebee, bumblebee,' asked the little foxes, 'can you tell us what snow is?' The bumblebee buzzed, carrying pollen.

'No time to waste,' she buzzed. 'I need to gather as much nectar as I can to make honey, because when the snow falls, I need plenty of energy to keep my queen bee warm until spring comes.' And with that, she hovered away.

'Frog, frog,' asked the little foxes, 'can you *please* tell us what the snow is?'

'I'm sorry little foxes, I can feel the icy-cold coming,' said frog, 'and I need to find a good place in the pond. When it comes, the top of the water will freeze to ice so I need to get to the bottom of the pond in time.'

And with a splash he jumped into the water and disappeared below.

'So snow makes food disappear, it's very cold, it falls from the sky and covers the ground and makes it hard, and it turns water to ice?' said the little foxes with amazement and bounded off to find someone else to tell them more.

But suddenly the rabbit came rushing by.

'Hurry home, little foxes,' she said breathlessly. 'It's getting late and frosty, the sun is setting and the snow is coming very soon now! Get back to your den and your mother's winter fur will keep you warm!'

And with two big bounces, she was gone.

The two little foxes went racing across the fields. The sun was beginning to set and it was getting bitingly cold.

After supper and sleepy now after their busy day, they snuggled up with Mother Fox, and fell fast asleep dreaming about all they'd been told about snow.

But as the sun rose, Mother Fox shook the little foxes awake. 'Come and look outside!' she said. The little foxes poked their noses out of the den and...

They gasped with delight.

'So this is snow!' they cried.

'It makes food disappear, it's very cold, it
falls from the sky, it covers the ground and
makes it hard, it turns water to ice, it's white...
and it looks like it will be fun to play in!'

And they played together all day
long until it was time to go to bed...

because they knew the snow would still be there to play in when they woke up in the morning.